To Monika and Luka

and those happy memories of trying
to catch crabs in the rain

www.davidmelling.co.uk

www.huglessdouglas.co.uk

HODDER CHILDREN'S BOOKS

First published in hardback in Great Britain in 2020
by Hodder and Stoughton
First published in paperback in 2021

Text and illustrations copyright © David Melling, 2020

The right of David Melling to be identified
as the author and illustrator of this Work has been
asserted by him in accordance with the Copyright,
Designs and Patents Act 1988.

A CIP catalogue record for this book
is available from the British Library.

HB ISBN: 978 1 444 92872 3
PB ISBN: 978 1 444 92871 6

13 5 7 9 10 8 6 4 2

Printed and bound in China

MIX
Paper from
responsible sources
FSC
www.fsc.org
FSC® C104740

Hodder Children's Books
An imprint of Hachette Children's Group
Part of Hodder and Stoughton
Carmelite House
50 Victoria Embankment
London, EC4Y 0DZ

An Hachette UK Company

www.hachette.co.uk
www.hachettechildrens.co.uk

HUGLESS DOUGLAS
and the
NATURE WALK

David Melling

Hodder
Children's
Books

Douglas was late.

He was rushing to put on his brand-new coat.
It was all zips and pockets so it was difficult
to hurry.

Douglas didn't want to be late for Little School's
first ever **Nature Walk.**

He arrived just in time to find Miss Moo-Hoo
handing out worksheets in the playground.

'This sheet has a list of animals,
plants and insects,' she trilled.

'When you find each one, tick the box,
bring it to me and I'll give you a sticker!'

Douglas was **SO** excited – he loved stickers!
He was even more excited when he spotted a
LADYBIRD on Little Bun's foot.

'Well done, Douglas!' said Miss Moo-Hoo.
'The first sticker goes to you!'

Soon, everyone was finding things from the list ...

tickly ANTS ...

shiny
BEETLES ...

jumping
GRASSHOPPERS ...

and slimy SNAILS.

'You've all found lovely bugs,' said Miss Moo-Hoo,
'but don't forget to look for **LEAVES, BERRIES** and ...'

'Miss, is this an ant?'
interrupted Patch.

'No, dear,' squeaked Miss Moo-Hoo,
'that's a s-spider …

Gosh, look at all those
LEGS!'

Douglas and Splosh found a hole – perfect for insects!
'I've found one already,' Douglas said.

'That's my toe!' snapped Rabbit. 'What **are** you doing?'

'We're finding things from this list,' said Douglas.
'Do you know where tadpoles live?'

'Well, they don't live in
my bath,' said Rabbit.
'Try Big Pond. It's that way ...'

Everyone else had already found

BIG POND!

Douglas and Splosh wasted no time grabbing
a fishing net and joining in.

Soon they had collected lots of tadpoles.
Everyone was so busy looking at their wriggly
new friends that they didn't notice the
DARK CLOUDS gathering overhead.

DRIP, DROP, DRIP, DROP...

'Oh dear – hoods up, everyone!' called Miss Moo-Hoo.
'I think it's starting to ...

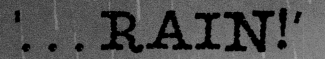

'...RAIN!'

Everyone dashed under a tree
for shelter. Big Pond got bigger ...
and bigger – until ...

'Oh dear,' said Miss Moo-Hoo.
'We're stranded! Whatever shall we do?'

'Quack!' said Splosh
happily.
'Quack, quack,
quack!'

'Look, there's my family!'
quacked Splosh. 'Mamma,
Papa! Over here!'

Splosh's family showed everyone how to
escape using the stepping stones.

But Douglas was only halfway across when
he heard someone calling his name …

It was a family of hedgehogs who had been collecting slugs. They were stranded too!

'Help us, Douglas! We're too small to jump across!'

He hurried back, scooped them up gently and carried them to safety.

'How can we thank you?' they asked.

'Can I borrow one of your slugs?'
Douglas asked the littlest hedgehog.

'It's the only thing
I haven't ticked
on my list.'

There were enough slugs for everyone!
'Oh, how lovely,' squeaked Miss Moo-Hoo.
'Well done, class.'

'Oh dear, my stickers are wet –
they've lost their stick!'
said Miss Moo-Hoo.

'Try this slug!'
said Woolly Sheep.
'It's super sticky!'

Miss Moo-Hoo shivered.
'Perhaps it's time to go.'

Back at Little School,
everyone huddled together
for a slimy, sticky …
'BUG HUG!'

HOW TO FIND INSECTS

Many insects eat leaves.

Lots of insects can fly, so look in the sky!

Ladybirds and lots of other insects like living on trees.

Caterpillars like hiding under leaves.

Worms live underground.

Snails, slugs and woodlice like to live in dark, moist places.

Some insects might come to you to say hello!

Spiders like making webs in your garden.

Bees and butterflies like to visit flowers.

Fish, tadpoles and water beetles live in ponds and streams.

You can find grasshoppers jumping in the long grass.

NATURE SPOT!

How many items on this list can you find?

Photocopy this page and take it with you on your next walk with family or friends.
It's a great way to look carefully at the lovely plants and creatures
that are all around you every day!

You can tick the correct boxes — or why not use some stickers, just like Douglas?

NATURE WALK CHECKLIST

	Ant			Leaf 1	
	Butterfly			Leaf 2	
	Worm			Leaf 3	
	Grasshopper			Berries	
	Spider			Pine cone	
	Caterpillar			Flower 1	
	Snail			Flower 2	
	Tadpole			Spider's web	
	Fish			Acorn	
	Water beetle			Feather	